# Contents

# Dramatis Personæ

**Romeo**
*Son to Montague*

**Chorus**
*Introduces the first two acts
of the play*

**Lord Montague**
*Head of the Montague house
(a Veronese family), at feud
with the Capulet family*

**Lady Montague**
*Wife to Montague*

**Benvolio**
*Nephew to Montague and friend
to Romeo and Mercutio*

**Balthasar**
*Servant to Romeo*

**Abraham**
*Servant to Montague*

**Escalus**
*Prince of Verona*

**Mercutio**
*Kinsman to Escalus, Prince of
Verona, and friend to Romeo
and Benvolio*

**Paris**
*A young nobleman, kinsman to
Escalus, Prince of Verona*

Juliet
*Daughter to Capulet*

Lord Capulet
*Head of the Capulet house
(a Veronese family), at feud
with the Montague family*

Lady Capulet
*Wife to Capulet*

Tybalt
*Nephew to Lady Capulet*

Nurse
*A Capulet servant and Juliet's
foster-mother*

Peter
*A Capulet servant to Juliet's nurse*

Sampson
*Servant to Capulet*

Gregory
*Servant to Capulet*

Friar Laurence
*A monk of the Franciscan Order*

Friar John
*A monk of the Franciscan Order*

# Romeo & Juliet

TWO RICH AND POWERFUL FAMILIES OF VERONA, THE MONTAGUES AND THE CAPULETS, RE-START AN OLD FEUD --

-- AND BLOOD IS SHED.

ROMEO *MONTAGUE* FALLS IN LOVE WITH JULIET *CAPULET.*

ALTHOUGH THEIR LOVE CAN **NEVER BE,** THEIR **DEATHS** BRING AN **END** TO THE FIGHTING.

Act I - Scene I

A PUBLIC PLACE IN VERONA – EARLY SUNDAY MORNING.

WE WON'T TAKE ANY NONSENSE FROM THEM, GREGORY.

NO, WE WON'T

WE'LL FIGHT THEM.

YOU WON'T RISK YOUR NECK!

I'M FAST WHEN I'M ANGRY.

WHEN'S THAT?

WHEN I SEE MONTAGUES.

YOU RUN AWAY WHEN YOU'RE ANGRY.

I'LL FIGHT ANY MONTAGUE.

YOU'RE A WIMP, SAMPSON.

I'LL FIGHT THE MEN AND PUSH THE GIRLS AROUND.

LEAVE THE GIRLS OUT OF IT.

I'LL CUT OFF THEIR HEADS!

THE GIRL'S HEADS?

YES, OR THEIR MAIDENHEADS – IF YOU PREFER.

WILL THEY FEEL IT?

THEY CERTAINLY WILL!

NOW'S YOUR CHANCE. HERE'S A COUPLE OF MONTAGUE'S MEN.

I'LL BACK YOU.

BY RUNNING AWAY?

DON'T WORRY ABOUT ME.

BUT I DO!

LET THEM START THE FIGHT.

I'LL GIVE THEM A DIRTY LOOK.

I'LL BITE MY THUMB AT THEM.

CLANG

OOF!

KTANGG

THUMP

STOP, YOU FOOLS!

PUT YOUR SWORDS AWAY.

FIGHTING WITH THE SERVANTS, BENVOLIO?

TURN ROUND AND PREPARE TO DIE!

I'M TRYING TO *STOP* THEM. WHY DON'T YOU HELP ME?

BECAUSE I HATE YOU, AND ALL MONTAGUES!

FIGHT, COWARD!

TA-TAN TA RA!

I'LL DEAL WITH **YOU** THIS AFTERNOON, MONTAGUE.

NOW MOVE *AWAY,* ALL OF YOU!

WHO **STARTED** THIS, NEPHEW?

THE SERVANTS. I TRIED TO STOP THEM, BUT **TYBALT** CAME ALONG, LOOKING FOR **TROUBLE.**

HE PULLED HIS **SWORD** ON ME. AS WE WERE **FIGHTING,** MORE PEOPLE GOT **INVOLVED** -- UNTIL THE **PRINCE** ARRIVED.

HE'S BEEN SEEN **CRYING** THERE **MANY** TIMES.

HE COMES BACK **HOME** WHEN IT GETS **LIGHT** AND LOCKS HIMSELF **AWAY** IN HIS ROOM.

I WISH I **KNEW** WHAT WAS **TROUBLING** HIM.

WON'T HE **TELL YOU**, UNCLE?

NO.

HAVE YOU TRIED TO **REASON** WITH HIM?

HE WON'T **TALK** TO **ANYONE**.

HE IS KEEPING IT ALL **BOTTLED** UP. IT ISN'T **GOOD** FOR HIM.

WE WOULD DO **ANYTHING** TO HELP HIM.

HERE HE IS!

LEAVE THIS TO **ME** – I'LL FIND OUT WHAT'S **WRONG** WITH HIM.

WHY AREN'T YOU LAUGHING?

I'M TOO SAD FROM SEEING YOU LIKE THIS.

I APPRECIATE YOUR CONCERN, BUT YOUR SADNESS ISN'T HELPING ME.

IT WOULD BE BETTER IF YOU LEFT ME ALONE.

LOVE IS A PUZZLE AND I JUST CAN'T UNDERSTAND IT.

FAREWELL, COUSIN.

LET ME COME WITH YOU.

COME WITH ME?

I'M NOT EVEN HERE MYSELF!

WHO ARE YOU IN LOVE WITH?

I DON'T WANT TO TALK ABOUT IT.

JUST TELL ME!

23

SHE IS WASTING HER BEAUTY.

HAS SHE PROMISED NEVER TO MARRY?

SHE HAS --

-- AND SO HER BEAUTY WILL NOT BE PASSED ON TO ANY CHILDREN.

IT'S UNFAIR THAT SOMEONE SO LOVELY AND WISE SHOULD MAKE ME SO MISERABLE.

FORGET ABOUT HER!

HOW?

25

THERE ARE PLENTY OF OTHER GIRLS.

NOT LIKE HER.

I CAN'T JUST SIMPLY FORGET ABOUT HER. ANY OTHER GIRL WOULD ONLY REMIND ME OF HER.

FAREWELL! YOU CAN'T MAKE ME FORGET HER.

I'LL FIND A WAY.

*A STREET IN VERONA – SUNDAY MORNING.*

MONTAGUE AND **I** MUST KEEP THE PEACE.

IT'S A **PITY** YOU HAVE BEEN ENEMIES FOR SO LONG.

NOW, MY LORD, WHAT DO YOU **SAY** TO MY REQUEST?

MY DAUGHTER IS STILL VERY **YOUNG**. SHE ISN'T EVEN **FOURTEEN** YET.

**MAYBE** IN A **YEAR** OR TWO.

**YOUNGER** GIRLS THAN **THAT** ARE MARRIED.

**EARLY** MARRIAGE CAN **RUIN** A GIRL. WHY DON'T YOU GET TO **KNOW** HER BETTER?

IF SHE **AGREES** TO MARRIAGE, THEN I WON'T STAND IN YOUR **WAY**.

I'M HAVING A **PARTY** HERE TONIGHT.

WHY DON'T **YOU** COME? THERE WILL BE **MANY** LOVELY GIRLS TO **DANCE** WITH.

WHEN YOU SEE THE **FINEST** YOUNG **LADIES** OF VERONA, YOU MIGHT **CHANGE** YOUR **MIND** ABOUT MY DAUGHTER.

MY MAN, GO ROUND **VERONA** AND **INVITE** THE PEOPLE ON THIS LIST TO MY PARTY **TONIGHT**.

HOW **CAN** I INVITE THE PEOPLE ON THIS **LIST?** I CAN'T **READ!**

I'LL HAVE TO **FIND** SOMEONE WHO **CAN**.

FIND YOURSELF SOMEONE **ELSE**. YOU'LL **SOON** FORGET ALL **ABOUT HER!**

I'LL **KICK** YOU IN A MINUTE!

ARE YOU **CRAZY?**

I MIGHT AS WELL BE --

GOOD AFTERNOON.

CAN YOU READ, SIR?

ONLY MY OWN FORTUNE.

CAN YOU READ WRITING?

AYE, IF I KNOW WHAT IT SAYS.

AH, THEN GOOD DAY, SIR.

WAIT! I CAN READ.

COUNT ANSELME, PLACENTIO, MERCUTIO, VALENTINE, TYBALT, ROSALINE -- THESE ARE INVITATIONS.

WHERE'S THE PARTY?

UP.

WHERE?

AT OUR HOUSE.

WHOSE HOUSE?

MY MASTER'S.

WHO IS YOUR MASTER?

THE GREAT RICH CAPULET.

WHY DON'T YOU COME ALONG - AS LONG AS YOU'RE NOT A MONTAGUE!

GOOD DAY!

SO! ROSALINE'S GOING TO BE AT THIS PARTY.

WE HAVE TO GO – THEN YOU CAN COMPARE HER TO THE OTHER GIRLS; AND I BET YOU WON'T THINK SHE'S SO BEAUTIFUL AFTER THAT!

THERE HAS NEVER BEEN A WOMAN MORE BEAUTIFUL THAN ROSALINE!

LET'S PROVE IT, THEN – AT CAPULET'S PARTY.

ALL RIGHT, I'LL GO – BUT ONLY BECAUSE ROSALINE WILL BE THERE.

THE CAPULETS' HOUSE – SUNDAY AFTERNOON.

NURSE, WHERE'S MY DAUGHTER?

CALL HER FOR ME.

I ASKED HER TO BE HERE.

JULIET!

WHO WANTS ME?

YOUR MOTHER.

31

WHAT'S THE MATTER?

LEAVE US ALONE FOR A WHILE, NURSE.

NO, WAIT - YOU SHOULD HEAR THIS TOO.

YOU KNOW MY DAUGHTER IS AT A CERTAIN AGE.

I KNOW HER EXACT AGE.

SHE' ISN'T FOURTEEN YET.

HOW LONG IS IT UNTIL AUGUST?

JUST OVER A FORTNIGHT.

SHE'LL BE FOURTEEN JUST BEFORE THEN - THE EXACT SAME AGE AS MY DEARLY DEPARTED DAUGHTER, SUSAN.

IT'S **ELEVEN** YEARS SINCE THE **EARTHQUAKE**. I'LL **NEVER** FORGET IT. WE WERE SITTING UNDER THE **DOVE-HOUSE** WALL --

-- EVERYTHING **SHOOK**, AND I RAN OUT AS **QUICKLY** AS I COULD.

THAT WAS **ELEVEN** YEARS AGO.

SHE COULD **STAND** ON HER **OWN** THEN, AND **RUN** ABOUT.

ONE DAY SHE **FELL** OVER AND **HURT** HER **HEAD** AND MY **HUSBAND** PICKED HER **UP** AND SAID,

"YOU'LL FALL ON YOUR **BACK** WHEN YOU'RE SMARTER, WON'T YOU JULE?"

SHE **STOPPED** CRYING AND SAID, "AYE."

I'LL NEVER FORGET IT! "WON'T YOU, JULE?", HE SAID -- AND SHE SAID, "AYE"!!

*ENOUGH!* BE QUIET!

BANG

33

YES, MADAM, BUT I CAN'T HELP **LAUGHING** WHEN I **THINK** ABOUT IT.

"YOU'LL FALL ON YOUR **BACK** WHEN YOU GROW UP," SAID MY HUSBAND,

AND SHE **STOPPED** CRYING AND SAID, "AYE."

AND **YOU** STOP TOO, NURSE. **PLEASE!**

I'M FINISHED! YOU WERE SUCH A PRETTY **BABY.**

I **DREAM** OF SEEING YOU **MARRIED** SOME DAY.

THAT'S WHAT I'VE COME TO **TALK** TO YOU ABOUT.

WOULD **YOU** LIKE TO GET **MARRIED,** JULIET?

IT'S AN HONOUR THAT I HAVEN'T REALLY **THOUGHT** ABOUT.

AN HONOUR! YOU **COULDN'T** HAVE GOT SUCH **WISDOM** FROM ME!

WELL, **THINK** ABOUT IT NOW.

GIRLS **YOUNGER** THAN YOU ARE **MARRIED.** I GAVE BIRTH TO **YOU** WHEN I WAS ABOUT **YOUR** AGE.

THE **HONOURABLE** COUNT **PARIS** WISHES TO **MARRY** YOU.

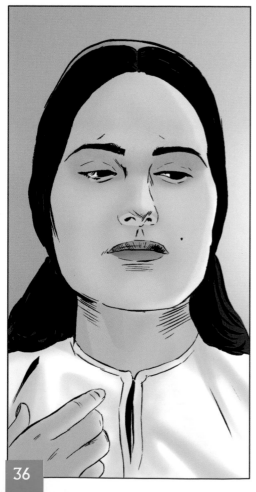

38

B·DUM B·DUM

41

Act I - Scene V

INSIDE THE CAPULETS' HOUSE – SUNDAY EVENING.

WHERE'S POTPAN?

IT'S NOT **RIGHT** THAT **WE** SHOULD BE DOING **ALL** THE **WORK!**

CLEAR AWAY THE **STOOLS** AND THE **PLATES.**

**ANTONY! POTPAN!**

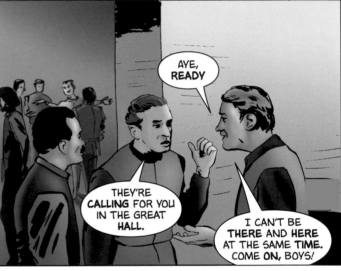

AYE, READY

THEY'RE **CALLING** FOR YOU IN THE GREAT **HALL.**

I CAN'T BE **THERE** AND **HERE** AT THE SAME **TIME.** COME **ON,** BOYS!

WELCOME, GENTLEMEN!

THE LADIES THAT **DON'T** HAVE **CORNS** ON THEIR **FEET** WILL **DANCE** WITH YOU.

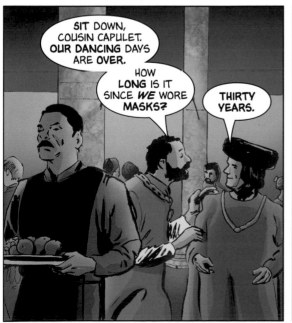

BUT HIS SON WAS JUST A CHILD TWO YEARS AGO!

WHO'S THAT GIRL DANCING WITH THAT NOBLEMAN OVER THERE?

I DON'T KNOW, SIR.

SHE IS SO BEAUTIFUL!

I'LL GO TO HER AFTER THIS DANCE. HOW COULD I THINK THAT I WAS IN LOVE BEFORE?

I've never seen true beauty until now.

THIS MAN IS A MONTAGUE!

FETCH MY SWORD, BOY.

44

BUT, UNCLE --

ENOUGH!

ENJOY, EVERYBODY!

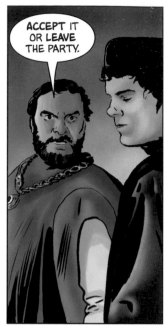
ACCEPT IT OR LEAVE THE PARTY.

MORE LIGHT!

DO WHAT I SAY.

ENJOY!

ALL RIGHT, I'LL GO. BUT THE MONTAGUES WILL PAY FOR THIS!

47

THERE: ALL MY **SIN** HAS GONE.

THEN MY LIPS NOW HAVE **YOUR** SIN.

LET ME TAKE IT BACK.

YOU KISS BY **LOGIC!**

MADAM, YOUR **MOTHER** WANTS A WORD.

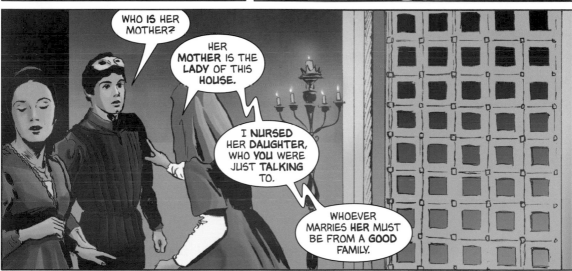

WHO IS HER MOTHER?

HER **MOTHER** IS THE LADY OF THIS HOUSE.

I NURSED HER **DAUGHTER,** WHO **YOU** WERE JUST **TALKING** TO.

WHOEVER MARRIES **HER** MUST BE FROM A **GOOD** FAMILY.

SHE'S A **CAPULET!** MY **LIFE** IS IN THE HANDS OF MY **ENEMY!**

LET'S LEAVE.

YES, LET'S.

THANK YOU FOR **COMING**, GENTLEMEN.

BRING MORE LIGHT HERE!

IT'S GETTING **LATE**. LET'S GO TO BED.

NURSE --

WHO IS THAT?

TIBERIO'S SON.

AND THAT MAN, THERE?

YOUNG PETRUCHIO.

AND HIM FOLLOWING?

I DON'T KNOW.

GO AND ASK HIS **NAME.** **PLEASE** TELL ME HE ISN'T ALREADY **MARRIED.**

HIS NAME IS **ROMEO;** AND HE'S A **MONTAGUE.**

How can the man I **love** be the **son** of those I hate?

It's so **unfair!**

WHAT'S WRONG?

NOTHING.

**JULIET!**

ONE MOMENT.

LET'S GO. EVERYBODY HAS LEFT.

Act II - Scene II

THE ORCHARD AT CAPULET'S HOUSE – PAST MIDNIGHT, MONDAY MORNING.

* Why are you Romeo?

59

FRIAR LAURENCE'S CHURCH, NEAR VERONA – EARLY MONDAY MORNING.

DAWN IS BREAKING.

I MUST FILL THIS BASKET WITH HERBS AND MEDICINAL PLANTS BEFORE THE SUN COMES UP.

THE EARTH GIVES US EVERYTHING – AND, WHEN THINGS DIE, THEY RETURN TO THE EARTH.

EVERY HERB AND PLANT IS DIFFERENT – SOME CAN HEAL, AND SOME CAN HARM – BUT ALL OF THEM HAVE A PURPOSE.

THERE'S **NOTHING** ON EARTH THAT DOESN'T HAVE **SOME** GOOD IN IT – BUT **EVERYTHING** CAN ALSO BE **MISUSED**.

THERE'S BOTH **POISON** AND **MEDICINE** INSIDE THIS SMALL **FLOWER**.

IT **SMELLS** SWEET, BUT YOU WOULD **DIE** IF YOU **ATE** IT.

THIS **MIX** OF **GOOD** AND **EVIL** IS IN **PEOPLE** AS WELL AS IN **PLANTS**.

GOOD MORNING, FATHER.

**ROMEO!** IT'S NOT LIKE **YOU** TO BE UP SO EARLY.

SOMETHING MUST BE **WRONG** – YOU HAVEN'T BEEN TO **BED** AT ALL, HAVE YOU?

YOU'RE **RIGHT**, I HAVEN'T.

GOD **FORGIVE** YOU!

WERE YOU WITH **ROSALINE?**

NO, FATHER – I'VE **FORGOTTEN** ALL ABOUT HER!

THAT'S **GOOD**.

BUT WHERE HAVE YOU BEEN?

AT A PARTY WITH MY ENEMY, WHERE I WAS **WOUNDED** BY SOMEONE WHO WAS ALSO **WOUNDED** BY ME. *ONLY YOU* CAN CURE US, FATHER.

IT WILL HELP MY **ENEMY** AS MUCH AS IT WILL HELP **ME**.

I DON'T UNDERSTAND –

I'M IN LOVE WITH **CAPULET'S** DAUGHTER!

WE'RE IN LOVE WITH EACH OTHER AND **NEED** TO GET MARRIED AS SOON AS POSSIBLE.

I'LL **TELL** YOU **ALL** ABOUT IT LATER –

PLEASE, MARRY US TODAY!

*HOLY SAINT FRANCIS!* HOW CAN YOU HAVE **FORGOTTEN** ROSALINE SO **SOON?**

YOUNG MEN **LOVE** WITH THEIR **EYES**, NOT WITH THEIR **HEARTS**.

HOW MANY **TEARS** DID YOU **SHED** FOR **ROSALINE?**

I CAN STILL **HEAR** YOUR SIGHS AND GROANS --

-- AND SEE THE TEAR STAINS ON YOUR CHEEKS.

DID YOU **REALLY** FEEL SO STRONGLY ABOUT **ROSALINE?**

HOW CAN ALL THAT HAVE CHANGED SO QUICKLY?

YOU TOLD ME OFF FOR LOVING ROSALINE.

FOR BEING OBSESSED WITH HER, YES.

YOU TOLD ME TO BURY MY LOVE.

YES - NOT TO EXCHANGE IT FOR ANOTHER!

PLEASE, DON'T LECTURE ME.

JULIET LOVES ME, AND ROSALINE DIDN'T!

THAT'S BECAUSE SHE KNEW YOU DIDN'T REALLY LOVE HER!

I WILL HELP YOU, FOR ONE REASON: THIS MIGHT BRING PEACE BETWEEN YOUR TWO FAMILIES.

THEN LET'S MOVE QUICKLY!

CRASH

WISELY AND SLOWLY - THOSE WHO RUN USUALLY FALL DOWN.

Act II - Scene IV

A STREET IN VERONA – MONDAY MORNING.

WHERE CAN ROMEO BE? DID HE COME **HOME** LAST NIGHT?

NOT TO HIS **FATHER'S** HOUSE.

THAT **ROSALINE'S** DRIVING HIM **CRAZY!**

**TYBALT** SENT A **LETTER** TO THE **MONTAGUE** HOUSE.

BANG

IT MUST BE A **CHALLENGE.**

ROMEO WILL **ANSWER** IT.

ANYONE WHO CAN WRITE CAN **ANSWER** A LETTER.

I MEAN, ROMEO WILL **FIGHT** HIM.

ROMEO'S ALREADY **DEAD** – KILLED BY HIS **LOVE** FOR **ROSALINE.**

HE'S NOT **FIT** TO FIGHT **TYBALT.**

WHAT'S SO **GREAT** ABOUT **TYBALT?**

HE'S A **TOP-CLASS SWORDSMAN!** HE KNOWS ALL THE **MOVES** – EVEN THE *HAI*!

THUD

THE **WHAT?**

THE KILLING THRUST! I HATE PEOPLE LIKE HIM: BIG-MOUTHS AND SHOW-OFFS!

HERE COMES ROMEO!

LIKE A LIMP FISH.

HE'LL ONLY TALK ABOUT HOW LOVELY ROSALINE IS.

SIGNOR ROMEO, YOU GAVE US THE SLIP LAST NIGHT.

GOOD MORNING! THE SLIP?

YOU KNOW WHAT I MEAN.

SORRY, MERCUTIO. I HAD SOME BUSINESS TO ATTEND TO.

YES – FUNNY BUSINESS! BENDING AT THE WAIST ...

YOU MEAN, CURTSY?

EXACTLY.

POLITELY PUT.

I'M THE VERY PINK OF POLITENESS.

MUCH TOO LITTLE FOR A LARGE LEG-PULLER.

ISN'T THIS BETTER?

YOU'RE ROMEO AGAIN, INSTEAD OF MOPING AROUND LIKE SOME LOVE-SICK IDIOT.

ENOUGH.

YOU WANT ME TO HOLD MY TALE?

YOUR LONG TALE --

WRONG! I WAS ALMOST FINISHED.

HERE'S GOOD SPORT!

A SAIL, A SAIL!

TWO! A SHIRT AND A SMOCK!

PETER!

MA'AM?

MY FAN, PETER.

YES, PETER – GIVE HER THE FAN TO HIDE HER FACE.

GOOD MORNING, GENTLEMEN.

GOOD AFTERNOON, DEAR LADY.

IS IT AFTERNOON?

IT IS. THE HAND OF THE CLOCK IS RIGHT UP THE MIDDLE OF NOON.

GET AWAY FROM ME! WHAT KIND OF MAN ARE YOU?

A MAN MADE BY GOD, AND RUINED BY SIN.

WHACK

GENTLEMEN, CAN YOU TELL ME WHERE I CAN FIND YOUNG ROMEO?

I CAN TELL YOU. I'M ROMEO.

GOOD.

IS IT GOOD?

IF YOU'RE ROMEO, I'D LIKE A PRIVATE WORD WITH YOU.

A PRIVATE WORD???

I'VE FOUND IT!

WHAT HAVE YOU FOUND?

AN OLD STALE HARE.

SWISH

♪ AN OLD STALE HARE, ISN'T GOOD ANYWHERE, IT SMELLS AND IT'S TOUGH, AND IT'S FAR TOO ROUGH! ♪

ROMEO, WE'RE OFF TO YOUR FATHER'S HOUSE FOR DINNER.

I'LL FOLLOW YOU.

FAREWELL, OLD LADY.

♪ LADY, LADY, LADY... ♪

FARE WELL!

WHO WAS THAT ROGUE?

SOMEONE WHO LOVES THE SOUND OF HIS OWN VOICE.

I'D TAKE HIM DOWN A PEG OR TWO!

I'M NOT ONE OF HIS LOOSE WOMEN, NOR ONE OF HIS DAGGER HOLDERS!

AND YOU STOOD BY AND LET HIM INSULT ME!

WHACK

HE DIDN'T INSULT YOU. I'D HAVE THREATENED HIM IF HE HAD.

I'M JUST AS BRAVE AS THE NEXT MAN!

I'M SHAKING WITH RAGE!

THE DIRTY SCOUNDREL!

SIR, AS I SAID, JULIET ASKED ME TO FIND YOU.

NOW, I HOPE YOU'RE NOT TRYING TO TAKE ADVANTAGE OF HER – SHE'S VERY YOUNG AND IT WOULD BE CRUEL OF YOU TO PLAY SUCH A DIRTY TRICK.

NURSE, I MUST PROTEST --

YOU'RE A GOOD MAN AND I'LL TELL HER THAT! SHE'LL BE VERY HAPPY.

WHAT WILL YOU TELL HER?

THAT YOU *"PROTEST"* -- THAT'S THE *GENTLEMANLY* THING TO DO.

JUST **TELL** HER TO GO TO FRIAR LAURENCE'S **CHURCH** THIS AFTERNOON.

TAKE **THIS** FOR YOUR **TROUBLE.**

NO, SIR. I WON'T TAKE A PENNY!

I INSIST.

**THIS** AFTERNOON, SIR? SHE'LL BE THERE.

IF YOU **WAIT** BEHIND THE ABBEY WALL, MY MAN WILL BRING YOU A **ROPE-LADDER.**

I'LL USE THAT **TONIGHT** TO CLIMB UP TO THE **ROOM** OF MY **DREAMS.**

**FAREWELL!** I SEND MY **LOVE** TO JULIET.

LISTEN, SIR --

WHAT IS IT?

CAN YOUR MAN BE TRUSTED?

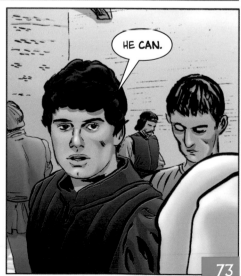

HE CAN.

73

Act II - Scene V

THE CAPULETS' GARDEN – MIDDAY, ON MONDAY.

THE *NURSE* SAID SHE'D BE *BACK* IN *HALF* AN HOUR.

WHAT'S *TAKING* HER SO *LONG*?

IT'S *THREE HOURS* SINCE SHE LEFT.

OLD PEOPLE ARE *SO SLOW.*

IF SHE WAS *YOUNGER* SHE'D MOVE *FASTER.*

OH, *HERE* SHE COMES!

DID YOU *SEE* HIM, NURSE?

WAIT HERE, PETER.

WHAT'S THE *MATTER*?

WHY IS YOUR FACE SO *SAD*? TELL ME THE *NEWS*, GOOD OR BAD.

I'M TIRED – GIVE ME A *MINUTE.* MY BONES *ACHE* FROM ALL THAT RUNNING ABOUT!

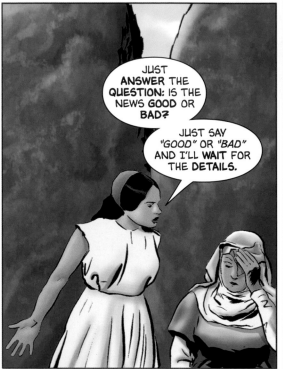

Act II - Scene VI

FRIAR LAURENCE'S CHURCH – MONDAY AFTERNOON.

MAY HEAVEN **BLESS** THIS HOLY **MARRIAGE.** I HOPE YOU DON'T LIVE TO REGRET THIS.

WE **WON'T.** NOTHING **BAD** CAN HAPPEN. IF I WERE TO **DIE** AS SOON AS WE ARE **MARRIED,** THEN I WOULD **DIE** A **HAPPY MAN.**

SUCH **PASSION** CAN LEAD TO A PASSIONATE **END.** TOO **FAST** IS JUST AS BAD AS TOO **SLOW.**

HERE COMES JULIET.

HOW LOVELY SHE LOOKS.

GOOD EVENING, GOOD FRIAR.

ROMEO IS READY, DEAR DAUGHTER.

AND SO AM I.

DEAR JULIET, IF YOU'RE AS HAPPY AS I AM NOW, IMAGINE HOW HAPPY WE WILL BE WHEN WE ARE MARRIED!

WORDS AREN'T ENOUGH TO DESCRIBE IT. MY LOVE IS SO GREAT, IT CANNOT BE MEASURED.

LET US BEGIN ...

Act III - Scene I

A PUBLIC PLACE IN VERONA – LATER, MONDAY AFTERNOON.

LET'S GO, MERCUTIO. THERE'S **TROUBLE** IN THE AIR. IF WE MEET UP WITH ANY **CAPULETS**, THERE'S **BOUND** TO BE A FIGHT. THIS **HOT** WEATHER MAKES PEOPLE **ANGRY**.

YOU'RE A BIT OF A TROUBLEMAKER **YOURSELF**, BENVOLIO.

AM I?

YOU LOSE YOUR **TEMPER** QUICKER THAN **ANY OTHER MAN** IN ITALY.

FOR WHAT REASON?

FOR ANY **REASON** --

-- THE LENGTH OF A MAN'S BEARD, THE COLOUR OF HIS EYES – ANYTHING!

YOUR BRAIN HAS BEEN SCRAMBLED BY FIGHTING.

YOU ONCE FOUGHT WITH A MAN WHO COUGHED AND WOKE YOUR DOG --

-- AND WITH ANOTHER WHOSE CLOTHES YOU DIDN'T LIKE!

CLUCK CLUCK

AND ANOTHER WHO USED OLD LACES TO TIE HIS NEW SHOES!

SO DON'T TALK TO ME ABOUT CONTROLLING MYSELF!

IF I WAS AS QUICK TO FIGHT AS YOU, MY LIFE WOULDN'T LAST LONG.

SQUAARK!

81

HERE COME THE CAPULETS.

I DON'T CARE!

STAY CLOSE. I'LL TALK TO THEM.

A WORD, PLEASE GENTLEMEN.

JUST ONE WORD? WHAT ABOUT A FIGHT AS WELL?

I CAN DO THAT TOO, IF YOU GIVE ME A REASON.

CAN'T YOU FIND A REASON ON YOUR OWN?

MERCUTIO, YOU'RE IN ROMEO'S GROUP –

GROUP?

WHAT ARE WE? MUSICIANS? GIVE ME MY SWORD – I'LL MAKE YOU DANCE!

ARGUE SOMEWHERE ELSE – THERE ARE TOO MANY PEOPLE WATCHING US HERE.

LET THEM WATCH! I'M GOING NOWHERE.

AH, HERE'S MY MAN!

HE'S NOT ONE OF *YOUR* MEN!.

ROMEO, YOU *VILLAIN!*

I'LL IGNORE THAT – I'M NO VILLAIN.

SO, FAREWELL – YOU DON'T **KNOW** ME AT ALL.

BUT I **WON'T** IGNORE THE INSULT YOU GAVE ME!

I NEVER INSULTED YOU. YOU **DON'T** UNDERSTAND HOW **MUCH** I RESPECT YOU, AND THE **NAME** OF CAPULET.

*IT'S NOT GOOD TO BACK DOWN LIKE THIS.*

83

I'LL **FIGHT** YOU, TYBALT!

WHY DO **YOU** WANT TO FIGHT **ME?**

I WANT ONE OF YOUR **NINE** LIVES, *KING OF CATS!* I MIGHT EVEN KNOCK THE **OTHER** EIGHT OUT OF YOU AS **WELL.**

DRAW YOUR SWORD!

I'LL **FIGHT** YOU.

PUT YOUR SWORD **AWAY,** MERCUTIO.

COME **ON,** LET'S **SEE** WHAT YOU'VE **GOT.**

*SWOOOOOOOOSH*

*STOP THEM, BENVOLIO!*

84

Why did you get **between** us, Romeo? He **wounded** me under **your** arm.

I WAS TRYING TO HELP --

Get me into some **house**, Benvolio, before I **faint**.

A PLAGUE O' BOTH YOUR HOUSES!

YOUR **FAMILIES** HAVE **KILLED** ME!

MERCUTIO IS MY **FRIEND**, AND A **RELATIVE** OF THE **PRINCE**. IT'S **MY** FAULT THAT HE'S BEEN **WOUNDED**.

OH **JULIET**, MY **LOVE** FOR **YOU** HAS MADE ME **WEAK**.

ROMEO! MERCUTIO'S DEAD!

THIS ISN'T THE **END** OF OUR MISERY ...

HERE'S **TYBALT** AGAIN.

HE'S **ALIVE**, AND MERCUTIO'S **DEAD**!

I'M TOO ANGRY TO BE PLEASANT!

TYBALT, YOU'RE THE VILLAIN NOW!

ONE OF US WILL BE GOING WITH MERCUTIO TO THE GRAVE!

YOU! YOU CAN JOIN HIM!

WE'LL SEE ABOUT THAT!

CLANG

AGHK

THUD

GET OUT OF HERE, ROMEO!

TYBALT'S DEAD AND THE OFFICERS ARE COMING. IF THEY CATCH YOU, YOU'LL BE EXECUTED.

I'M SUCH A FOOL!

GO!

WHICH WAY DID MERCUTIO'S KILLER, TYBALT, GO?

HE'S LYING OVER THERE.

YOU, COME WITH ME – IN THE NAME OF THE PRINCE.

A FEW MINUTES LATER...

WHO STARTED THIS FIGHT?

NOBLE PRINCE --

-- TYBALT KILLED MERCUTIO, AND THEN ROMEO KILLED TYBALT.

OH! MY LOVELY NEPHEW, TYBALT, HAS BEEN KILLED!

OH, HE IS *DEAD!*

PLEASE, PRINCE, YOU **MUST** MAKE A **MONTAGUE** PAY FOR THIS **MURDER** – WITH HIS *LIFE!*

OH, MY **NEPHEW!**

BENVOLIO, WHO **STARTED** THIS FIGHT?

TYBALT.

ROMEO **TRIED** TO **STOP** HIM, BUT HE WOULDN'T **LISTEN.** HE **DREW** HIS **SWORD** AND POINTED IT AT MERCUTIO'S **HEART.**

MERCUTIO BECAME **ANGRY** AND A **FIGHT** BEGAN.

ROMEO **TRIED** TO BREAK IT UP AND GOT **BETWEEN** THEM.

THEN, TYBALT REACHED **UNDER** ROMEO'S ARM AND **THRUST** HIS SWORD INTO **MERCUTIO** – AND RAN **AWAY.**

ROMEO WANTED **REVENGE.** WHEN TYBALT CAME **BACK,** THEY BEGAN **FIGHTING.**

TYBALT WAS **DEAD** BEFORE I COULD GET **BETWEEN** THEM.

BANG BANG

89

HE'S A MONTAGUE – HE'S BOUND TO LIE FOR THEM.

IT TOOK TWENTY OF THEM TO KILL TYBALT!

I DEMAND JUSTICE, PRINCE. ROMEO MUST DIE!

ROMEO KILLED TYBALT, BECAUSE TYBALT KILLED MERCUTIO. WHO WILL PAY FOR MERCUTIO'S LIFE?

NOT ROMEO, PRINCE – HE WAS MERCUTIO'S FRIEND.

BY KILLING TYBALT, HE ONLY DID WHAT THE LAW WOULD HAVE DONE.

AND FOR THAT OFFENCE HE MUST LEAVE VERONA IMMEDIATELY!

MERCUTIO WAS PART OF MY FAMILY. NOW, I HAVE BEEN AFFECTED BY YOUR FIGHTING –

YOU'LL ALL PAY DEARLY FOR THIS.

TELL ROMEO TO LEAVE THE CITY AT ONCE.

IF HE IS FOUND HERE AGAIN, HE WILL BE EXECUTED.

IF YOU SAY *"AYE"*, THEN I WILL DIE TOO.

IF HE'S **DEAD**, SAY *"AYE"*. IF **NOT**, SAY *"NO"*.

I SAW THE **WOUND** WITH MY OWN EYES –

HE WAS AS PALE AS ASHES AND COVERED IN BLOOD. I FAINTED AT THE SIGHT.

MY HEART IS BROKEN! I'LL KILL MYSELF!

OH TYBALT! YOU WERE MY BEST FRIEND!

WHAT ARE YOU SAYING?

IS **TYBALT** DEAD AS WELL AS ROMEO?

ROMEO KILLED **TYBALT** – AND NOW ROMEO IS BANISHED FROM VERONA.

OH MY LORD! WHY WOULD ROMEO KILL TYBALT?

*CURSE THE DAY!*

HOW COULD HE BEHAVE LIKE SUCH A MONSTER?

HOW COULD I **NOT SEE** THIS **WICKEDNESS** IN HIM?

HOW COULD A **HORRIBLE BOOK** HAVE SUCH A **LOVELY COVER?** HOW COULD **NATURE** MAKE SUCH A **FIEND?**

NO MAN CAN BE TRUSTED.

WHERE'S PETER? I NEED SOME BRANDY.

**SHAME** ON **ROMEO!**

NO – DON'T SAY SUCH A THING.

I KNOW ROMEO IS A GOOD MAN – I KNOW IT –

OH, HOW COULD I SAY WHAT I DID ABOUT HIM?

HE KILLED YOUR **COUSIN!**

-- BUT, TO **FOLLOW** WITH *"ROMEO IS **BANISHED**"* IS LIKE SAYING MY FATHER **AND** MOTHER, TYBALT, ROMEO **AND** JULIET ARE **ALL** DEAD.

**NOTHING** COULD BE **WORSE!**

**WHERE ARE** MY **PARENTS**, NURSE?

**GRIEVING** OVER TYBALT'S **BODY.**

I'LL **TAKE** YOU **TO** THEM.

WHEN ALL **THEIR** TEARS ARE DRY, I'LL **STILL** BE CRYING FOR **ROMEO.**

NURSE, **TAKE** THE **ROPE-LADDER AWAY.**

IT WON'T BE **NEEDED** NOW. WE HAVE **BOTH** LOST WHO WE WERE **MADE** FOR.

I'M **GOING** TO BED -- WHERE **DEATH**, NOT ROMEO, SHALL **TAKE** ME.

STAY IN YOUR **ROOM.** I **KNOW** WHERE ROMEO IS -- I'LL **GET** HIM FOR YOU.

PLEASE **FIND** HIM AND GIVE HIM **THIS** RING. TELL HIM TO COME **HERE** AND SAY HIS LAST **FAREWELL.**

FRIAR LAURENCE'S CHURCH – MONDAY NIGHT.

SHOW YOURSELF, ROMEO.

YOU ALWAYS SEEM TO BE IN TROUBLE.

WHAT NEWS, FATHER?

I HAVE NEWS OF THE PRINCE'S SENTENCE.

IS IT DEATH?

NO – THE SENTENCE WAS BANISHMENT.

BANISHMENT?

THAT'S EVEN WORSE THAN DEATH!

YOU'RE ONLY BANISHED FROM VERONA – THE WORLD IS A BIG PLACE.

97

THERE IS NO WORLD OUTSIDE VERONA! *BANISHMENT* IS JUST *DEATH* BY ANOTHER NAME --

-- IT'S THE SAME AS KILLING ME.

HOW *UNGRATEFUL!* WHAT YOU *DID* CARRIES THE *DEATH* SENTENCE, BUT THE PRINCE HAS *BANISHED* YOU INSTEAD --

-- AND YOU'RE *STILL* NOT *HAPPY.*

HE HASN'T SHOWN ME ANY MERCY.

I WANT TO BE *HERE,* WHERE JULIET IS.

EVERY LIVING *CREATURE* UNDER THE *SUN* CAN *STAY* IN VERONA AND BE WITH JULIET,

BUT *I* CAN'T!

AND *YOU* SAY BANISHMENT IS BETTER THAN DEATH?

KILL ME WITH SOMETHING ELSE, OTHER THAN *BANISHMENT!*

HOW CAN YOU EVEN SAY THAT *FATAL* WORD TO ME?

*"BANISHED?"*

SMAASH!

LISTEN TO ME --

*NO!* YOU'LL ONLY TALK ABOUT BANISHMENT.

I CAN GIVE YOU **ADVICE** TO HELP YOU.

CAN YOUR ADVICE **CREATE** A JULIET, OR **MOVE** A CITY, OR **REVERSE** A PRINCE'S SENTENCE?

IF IT **CAN'T**, THEN IT'S OF **NO USE** TO ME.

MADMEN NEVER LISTEN --

-- AND WISE MEN CANNOT SEE!

LET ME EXPLAIN.

YOU CANNOT TALK ABOUT SOMETHING THAT YOU DON'T UNDERSTAND!

YOU'RE NOT YOUNG AND IN LOVE LIKE I AM!

KNOCK KNOCK

GET UP, SOMEONE'S KNOCKING.

HIDE!

NO – LET THE MISTY BREATH FROM MY BROKEN HEART HIDE ME.

KNOCK KNOCK

LISTEN TO THEM KNOCKING!

KNOCK KNOCK

WHO'S THERE?

ROMEO, GET UP –

–– YOU'LL BE ARRESTED.

KNOCK KNOCK

WAIT!

RUN TO MY STUDY.

KNOCK KNOCK

WAIT A MINUTE!

HURRY!

100

KNOCK KNOCK KNOCK KNOCK

WHO IS IT? WHAT DO YOU WANT?

LET ME **IN** – I HAVE COME FROM LADY JULIET.

THEN YOU ARE WELCOME.

WHERE'S ROMEO?

LYING ON THE GROUND, CRYING.

HE'S ACTING **JUST LIKE** JULIET!

THIS IS PITIFUL!

SHE'S JUST LIKE THIS – BLUBBERING AND CRYING.

STAND UP AND BE A MAN! GET UP FOR JULIET'S SAKE!

*NURSE!*

YOU **CAN'T** JUST LIE THERE!

HOW IS JULIET? **WHERE** IS SHE? WHAT DOES SHE SAY?

SHE SAYS **NOTHING.** SHE JUST **CRIES** AND CALLS OUT *"TYBALT"* AND *"ROMEO."*

IT'S ALL MY FAULT!

TELL ME, FRIAR, **WHERE** IN MY **BODY** DOES MY **NAME** LIVE?

TELL ME, SO I CAN **CUT IT OUT!**

DON'T DO IT!

COME ON, BEHAVE LIKE A MAN!

I THOUGHT YOU WERE MORE **SENSIBLE** THAN THIS.

BY **KILLING** YOURSELF, YOU'LL **ALSO** BE KILLING YOUR **WIFE** – BECAUSE SHE LIVES **ONLY** FOR YOU.

*Fling...*

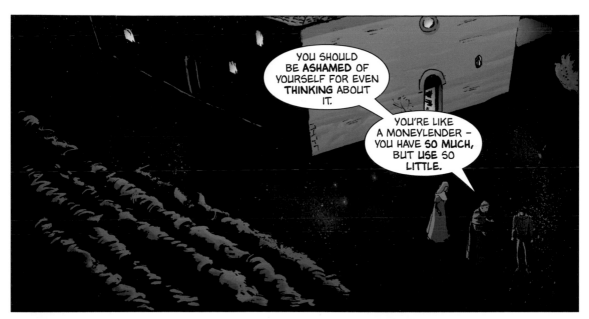

103

BUT HERE **YOU** ARE, COMPLAINING LIKE A SULKY **CHILD.**

**PEOPLE** WHO DO **THAT** USUALLY DIE **SAD** AND **LONELY.**

GO TO **JULIET,** LIKE WE **PLANNED;** BUT DON'T STAY TOO **LONG,** OR THE TOWN **GUARDS** WILL **STOP** YOU FROM **ESCAPING** TO **MANTUA.**

**THAT'S** WHERE YOU MUST **LIVE** --

-- UNTIL WE CAN **SORT** ALL THIS **OUT** AND GET YOU BACK **HERE** AGAIN.

GO ON **AHEAD** OF HIM, NURSE - GIVE MY **REGARDS** TO JULIET AND TELL HER **ROMEO** IS **COMING.**

YOU'RE A **WONDERFUL MAN,** FATHER.

**ROMEO,** I'LL TELL **JULIET** YOU'LL BE **THERE.**

THE CAPULETS' HOUSE – MONDAY NIGHT.

THE WAY THINGS HAVE **BEEN**, WE HAVEN'T HAD **TIME** TO **CONVINCE** JULIET TO **MARRY** YOU.

SHE **LOVED** TYBALT VERY **MUCH**, AS DID I.

IT'S **LATE** NOW – SHE WON'T **COME DOWN** TONIGHT.

I UNDERSTAND.

GOODNIGHT, MADAM. GIVE MY **REGARDS** TO JULIET.

I WILL.

**WAIT!** COUNT PARIS ... WHY DON'T I **OFFER** YOU MY DAUGHTER'S **HAND** ON HER **BEHALF?**

I'M **SURE** SHE'LL **AGREE** TO MY **DECISION.**

LET'S **ARRANGE** THE WEDDING FOR **WEDNESDAY.**

WAIT ... WHAT DAY IS IT TODAY?

MONDAY.

MONDAY? THEN WEDNESDAY IS TOO **SOON**. MAKE IT THURSDAY.

CAN YOU BE **READY**? WE'LL JUST INVITE A FEW FRIENDS.

IT WOULD BE **WRONG** OF US TO HAVE A BIG **PARTY** SO **SOON** AFTER TYBALT'S **DEATH**.

WHAT DO YOU SAY TO **THURSDAY**?

I WISH IT WAS THURSDAY **TOMORROW**.

THURSDAY IT IS, THEN.

GO TO JULIET, DEAR WIFE, AND MAKE SURE SHE IS **READY** FOR MARRIAGE.

FAREWELL, COUNT.

LIGHT THE WAY TO MY **BEDROOM**! IT'S SO **LATE**, IT WILL SOON BE **MORNING**!

THE CAPULETS' HOUSE – JULIET'S CHAMBER, EARLY TUESDAY MORNING.

DO YOU HAVE TO GO?

IT'S NOT **MORNING** YET. THAT WAS THE **NIGHTINGALE** YOU HEARD, NOT THE LARK.

LOOK, MY LOVE, DAWN IS **BREAKING** – IT'S ALMOST **DAY**.

I HAVE TO GO, OR I'LL BE **KILLED**.

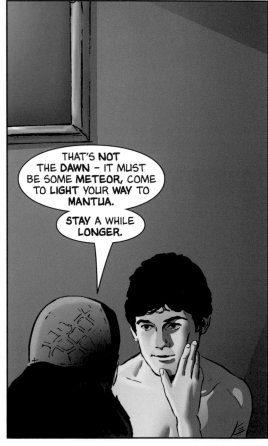

THAT'S **NOT** THE DAWN – IT MUST BE SOME **METEOR**, COME TO **LIGHT** YOUR **WAY** TO MANTUA.

**STAY** A WHILE LONGER.

IF **THAT'S** WHAT YOU **WANT** – I DON'T **CARE** IF I GET **ARRESTED** AND **EXECUTED**.

I'LL PRETEND IT'S **NOT** MORNING. I HAVE **MORE** REASON TO **STAY** THAN TO **LEAVE**.

111

HE IS **NO** VILLAIN.

PERHAPS YOU ARE **CRYING** BECAUSE THAT VILLAIN IS STILL **ALIVE**.

WHAT VILLAIN?

ROMEO.

GOD FORGIVE HIM!

I DO, YET THERE IS NO OTHER MAN WHO UPSETS ME MORE.

THAT'S BECAUSE HE IS STILL ALIVE.

AYE, AND BECAUSE HE IS BEYOND MY REACH.

WE WILL HAVE OUR **REVENGE**, DON'T WORRY.

I'LL GET SOMEONE IN MANTUA TO POISON HIM. WILL **THAT** SATISFY YOU?

I'LL **NEVER** BE SATISFIED UNTIL I **SEE** ROMEO – **DEAD** – MY HEART IS, **BROKEN** BY MY COUSIN.

I WILL MIX THE POISON *MYSELF* SO THAT ROMEO WILL SLEEP SOUNDLY WHEN HE TAKES IT.

I WANT TO GET **NEAR** TO ROMEO – TO **INFLICT** THE **LOVE** I HAD FOR **TYBALT** ON THE **BODY** OF THE MAN WHO **KILLED** HIM.

WE WILL **FIND A WAY.** BUT **NOW,** I HAVE SOME **HAPPY** NEWS FOR YOU.

GOOD! I COULD DO WITH SOME JOY.

YOUR FATHER HAS ARRANGED A **SURPRISE** – TO TAKE YOUR MIND OFF YOUR **SORROW.**

WHEN FOR?

**THURSDAY** MORNING, AT SAINT PETER'S CHURCH, YOU ARE TO BE MARRIED TO COUNT **PARIS.**

**NO!** I WON'T MARRY HIM!

I DON'T EVEN **KNOW** HIM.

TELL MY **FATHER** THAT I'M NOT **READY** TO GET **MARRIED** YET --

-- AND, WHEN I **DO**, IT WON'T BE TO **PARIS**. I'D RATHER MARRY **ROMEO** --

-- **WHOM** I **HATE**.

HERE COMES YOUR **FATHER**. YOU CAN TELL HIM YOURSELF.

WHAT'S **THIS**? ARE YOU STILL **CRYING**, GIRL?

YOUR **EYES** ARE LIKE LITTLE **BOATS**, BEING TOSSED ABOUT ON A **SEA** OF **TEARS**.

HAVE YOU **TOLD** HER, DEAR WIFE?

I **HAVE**, BUT SHE WON'T **AGREE** TO IT. I WISH THIS **FOOLISH** GIRL WAS **DEAD**!

WHAT DO YOU **MEAN**, SHE WON'T **AGREE** TO IT?

ISN'T SHE **GRATEFUL** THAT WE HAVE **ARRANGED** SUCH A GOOD MARRIAGE FOR HER?

I AM GRATEFUL, BUT --

SHAME ON YOU! WHAT, ARE YOU CRAZY?

DEAR FATHER, I BEG YOU!

LET ME SPEAK --

BUT WHAT?

"THANKS, BUT NO THANKS"?

YOU STILL LIVE UNDER MY ROOF! YOU'LL BE IN SAINT PETER'S CHURCH NEXT THURSDAY, EVEN IF I HAVE TO DRAG YOU THERE MYSELF!

I'M ASHAMED OF YOU, YOU GOOD-FOR-NOTHING LITTLE BRAT.

CRASH

TO HELL WITH YOU, YOU WORTHLESS WRETCH!

MARRY PARIS ON THURSDAY, OR NEVER LOOK ME IN THE FACE AGAIN.

NOW DON'T ANSWER ME BACK, OR I'LL STRIKE YOU!

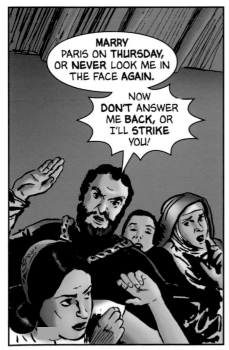

WE THOUGHT WE WERE UNLUCKY NOT HAVING MORE THAN ONE CHILD, BUT NOW I SEE THAT EVEN THIS ONE IS ONE TOO MANY!

YOU'RE WRONG TO SAY SUCH THINGS ABOUT HER.

115

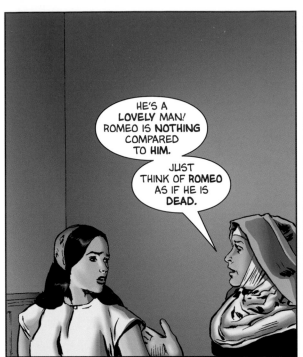

HE'S A LOVELY MAN! ROMEO IS **NOTHING** COMPARED TO HIM.

JUST THINK OF ROMEO AS IF HE IS **DEAD**.

IS THAT **REALLY** WHAT YOU **THINK?**

IN MY **HEART** AND **SOUL** — OR **CURSE** THEM BOTH.

**AMEN!**

WHAT?

THANK YOU FOR YOUR **ADVICE** —

— **TELL MY** MOTHER THAT I'VE GONE TO FRIAR LAURENCE TO ASK **FORGIVENESS** FOR MAKING MY FATHER ANGRY.

IT'S THE **RIGHT** THING TO DO.

*WICKED* OLD WITCH! I'LL *NEVER* TRUST HER WITH MY *SECRETS* AGAIN.

*THE FRIAR* WILL ADVISE ME. IF ALL *ELSE* FAILS, I CAN ALWAYS *KILL* MYSELF.

FRIAR LAURENCE'S CHURCH – TUESDAY MORNING.

ON **THURSDAY**, SIR? THAT'S VERY **SOON**.

**THAT'S** WHEN CAPULET **WANTS** IT.

BUT YOU DON'T **KNOW** WHAT JULIET **THINKS**, YET.

SHE IS STILL **GRIEVING** OVER **TYBALT**, AND I HAVEN'T BEEN **ABLE** TO **TALK** TO HER.

HER **FATHER** THINKS IT IS **DANGEROUS** FOR HER TO BE SO **UNHAPPY** --

-- AND SO WE SHOULD GET MARRIED **QUICKLY** TO MAKE HER **HAPPY** AGAIN. NOW YOU KNOW WHY WE **NEED** TO HURRY.

AND I **ALSO** KNOW WHY IT **SHOULDN'T** GO AHEAD.

HERE COMES JULIET NOW --

=grasp=

MY LADY ... MY **WIFE!**

I'M **NOT** YOUR WIFE YET.

YOU WILL BE, ON **THURSDAY.**

WHAT WILL BE, WILL **BE.**

VERY **TRUE.**

119

HAVE YOU COME TO MAKE **CONFESSION** TO THE **FRIAR**?

TO **HIM**, AND **NOT** TO YOU!

TELL HIM THAT YOU **LOVE** ME.

I'LL TELL **YOU** THAT I LOVE **HIM**.

I'M **SURE** YOU'LL SAY THAT YOU LOVE **ME** TOO.

IF I **DO**, IT WOULD BE **BEST** SAID WHEN YOU'RE **NOT** HERE.

YOUR **FACE** LOOKS LIKE IT HAS BEEN **CRYING**.

IT **ALWAYS** LOOKS LIKE THAT.

NO – DON'T **SAY** THAT!

IT'S THE **TRUTH**.

YOUR **FACE** IS **MINE**, AND YOU ARE **INSULTING** IT.

**MAYBE** – MY FACE IS NO **LONGER** MY OWN.

DO YOU HAVE TIME **NOW**, HOLY FATHER, OR SHALL I COME BACK **LATER**?

I HAVE TIME **NOW**.

PLEASE **EXCUSE** US.

OF COURSE.

JULIET, I WILL **CALL** FOR YOU **EARLY** ON **THURSDAY** MORNING.

**FAREWELL**, UNTIL THEN.

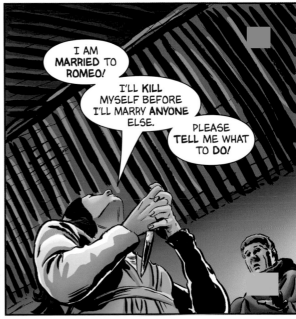

WOULD YOU!?

I WOULD DO *ANYTHING* TO AVOID MARRYING PARIS!

ANYTHING! TO BE ABLE TO LIVE AS A FAITHFUL WIFE TO MY SWEET LOVE.

VERY WELL, THEN. GO HOME AND LOOK HAPPY. AGREE TO MARRY PARIS.

MAKE SURE YOU ARE ALONE TOMORROW NIGHT AND DRINK THIS WHEN YOU GO TO BED.

YOU WILL FALL INTO A DEEP, DEEP SLEEP. YOU WILL HAVE NO PULSE, YOUR BODY WILL GO COLD, AND YOU WILL STOP BREATHING.

YOU WILL APPEAR TO BE *DEAD*.

THIS WILL LAST FORTY-TWO HOURS. THEN YOU WILL WAKE UP, AND BE BACK TO NORMAL.

THE CAPULETS' HOUSE – TUESDAY EVENING.

INVITE EVERYONE ON THIS LIST.

GET ME TWENTY GOOD COOKS.

I WILL ASK THEM TO LICK THEIR FINGERS.

WHY?

IF A COOK WON'T LICK HIS OWN FINGERS, HE'S NOT VERY GOOD.

HURRY – WE HAVEN'T MUCH TIME.

HAS JULIET GONE TO FRIAR LAURENCE?

YES.

WELL, I HOPE HE CAN MAKE THAT STUBBORN WENCH SEE SENSE.

HERE SHE COMES.

WHERE HAVE YOU BEEN?

FRIAR LAURENCE TOLD ME TO KNEEL BEFORE YOU AND BEG YOUR PARDON.

PLEASE FORGIVE ME – I AM READY TO DO WHATEVER YOU WANT.

124

SEND FOR THE COUNT.

WE SHALL **HAVE** THIS WEDDING TOMORROW MORNING!

I MET COUNT **PARIS** AT FRIAR LAURENCE'S **CHURCH**, AND I GAVE HIM MY **LOVING** RESPECT.

THIS IS **GOOD** – THIS IS HOW IT SHOULD BE!

BRING THE COUNT HERE.

WE OWE A **LOT** TO THIS FRIAR.

NURSE, WILL YOU **HELP** ME TO CHOOSE MY CLOTHES?

THERE'S PLENTY OF TIME BEFORE THURSDAY.

THE WEDDING WILL NOW BE TOMORROW!

WE WON'T BE **READY** IN TIME!

I'LL SORT **EVERYTHING** OUT, EVEN IF I HAVE TO STAY UP ALL NIGHT.

YOU GO WITH JULIET.

EVERYONE'S **GONE!** OH WELL, I'LL GO TO THE COUNT **MYSELF** – AND MAKE SURE HE IS **READY** FOR TOMORROW.

125

127

THE CAPULETS' HOUSE – EARLY WEDNESDAY MORNING.

FETCH MORE **SPICES**, NURSE.

THEY'RE SHOUTING FOR **INGREDIENTS** IN THE **KITCHEN**.

COME ON, **STIR** YOURSELVES!

IT'S **THREE** O'CLOCK!

GO TO **BED**, OR YOU'LL BE ILL TOMORROW.

NOT AT **ALL!** I'VE STAYED UP **ALL NIGHT** BEFORE.

OH YES, YOU KNEW HOW TO **PARTY** WHEN YOU WERE **YOUNGER**, BUT **I'M** KEEPING MY **EYE** ON YOU NOW!

YOU'RE **JEALOUS!**

WHAT DO YOU HAVE **THERE?**

THINGS FOR THE **COOK**, SIR.

BE QUICK! BE **QUICK!**

129

THE CAPULETS' HOUSE – JULIET'S CHAMBER, WEDNESDAY MORNING.

Mistress! Juliet! Fast asleep, I'll bet.

SWEETHEART!

BRIDE!

KNOCK KNOCK KNOCK

THAT'S RIGHT, GET ALL THE SLEEP YOU CAN! YOU WON'T BE GETTING MUCH REST TONIGHT!

SHE'S SOUND ASLEEP – I'LL HAVE TO WAKE HER.

JULIET!

WHAT, DRESSED AND LYING BACK DOWN AGAIN?

I HAVE TO WAKE YOU.

LADY! LADY! LADY!

OH MY WORD!

HELP!

MY LADY IS DEAD!

MY LORD! MY LADY!

IS THE BRIDE READY TO GO TO CHURCH?

READY TO GO, BUT NEVER TO RETURN.

OH PARIS, YOUR BRIDE HAS DIED ON THE NIGHT BEFORE YOUR WEDDING DAY.

MY DAUGHTER IS MARRIED TO DEATH. DEATH IS MY NEW SON-IN-LAW, AND MY ONLY HEIR.

I HAVE LOOKED FORWARD TO THIS MORNING; BUT NOW, THIS!

WHAT A TERRIBLE DAY!

I ONLY HAD ONE CHILD – MY ONLY SOURCE OF HAPPINESS AND HOPE.

AND NOW CRUEL DEATH HAS SNATCHED HER AWAY FROM ME.

WHAT A MISERABLE, MISERABLE DAY!

WHAT A DARK, HATEFUL DAY!

I HAVE BEEN TRICKED – DIVORCED, WRONGED AND HARMED – BY DEATH!

OH MY LOVE! MY LIFE! GONE! BUT STILL MY LOVE IN DEATH!

WHY HAS THIS HAPPENED?

WHY HAS DEATH COME TO RUIN OUR PLANS?

OH MY CHILD! MY CHILD IS DEAD! AND ALL MY HOPES AND DREAMS ARE BURIED WITH HER.

PEACE! BE CALM!

THIS WAILING WON'T HELP YOU. JULIET HAS GONE TO HEAVEN, WHERE SHE HAS BEEN GRANTED ETERNAL LIFE.

SHE IS IN A BETTER PLACE – HIGHER THAN THE LIFE YOU HAD PLANNED FOR HER, HERE ON EARTH.

YOU CRY, YET SHE IS PERFECTLY WELL THERE.

DRY YOUR TEARS, AND WE WILL TAKE HER TO THE CHURCH.

I KNOW IT IS NATURAL TO GRIEVE, BUT YOU REALLY SHOULD BE HAPPY FOR HER.

THE WEDDING CELEBRATIONS MUST NOW BECOME A SAD FUNERAL.

EVERYTHING IS THE OPPOSITE OF WHAT IT WAS.

EVERYONE, **PREPARE** FOR THE **FUNERAL**.

**HEAVEN** IS ALREADY **ANGRY** – DON'T MAKE THINGS **WORSE** BY GOING AGAINST **GOD'S** WILL.

WE MIGHT AS WELL **LEAVE**.

PUT YOUR INSTRUMENTS **AWAY** – THEY'RE NOT **NEEDED** HERE.

AYE, THINGS ARE **BAD**.

MUSICIANS, PLEASE PLAY *"HEART'S EASE"*.

WHY?

PLAY SOME **CHEERFULLY** SAD SONG – TO **COMFORT** ME.

NOW IS **NOT** THE TIME TO PLAY.

YOU **WON'T** PLAY?

NO.

THEN, I'LL GIVE IT TO **YOU**.

WHAT?

NO MONEY, JUST AN INSULT! *MINSTREL!*

THEN, I'LL CALL YOU *SERVANT!*

135

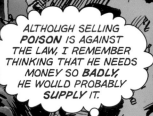

ALTHOUGH SELLING *POISON* IS AGAINST THE LAW, I REMEMBER THINKING THAT HE NEEDS MONEY SO *BADLY*, HE WOULD PROBABLY *SUPPLY* IT.

I'M *SURE* HE WILL SELL SOME POISON TO ME.

*THIS IS* THE *PLACE*. IT'S *SHUT* FOR THE HOLIDAY.

OPEN UP!

BANG BANG

WHO'S THERE?

COME HERE, MAN.

CREEAK

I KNOW YOU ARE POOR AND NEED *MONEY*.

I WANT POISON – *STRONG* POISON.

I *HAVE* IT, BUT IT'S AGAINST THE *LAW* TO SELL IT.

WHAT DO *YOU* CARE ABOUT THE LAW? THE LAW DOES *NOTHING* TO HELP YOU – BUT I WILL.

TAKE THIS MONEY AND *BREAK* THE LAW.

ALL *RIGHT* – BUT IT DOESN'T MAKE *THIS* RIGHT.

GOOD MAN.

TAKE THIS. IT WILL *KILL* YOU INSTANTLY.

HERE'S YOUR MONEY --

-- AND **THAT'S** A **WORSE** POISON THAN **ANYTHING** YOU COULD SELL TO ME.

*CHINK KA-CHINK KA-CHINK CHINK*

FAREWELL! BUY YOURSELF SOME **FOOD** AND PUT SOME **MEAT** ON YOUR **BONES**.

THE POISON YOU HAVE SOLD IS **MEDICINE** TO ME, THAT WILL TAKE ME TO **JULIET**!

FRIAR LAURENCE'S CHURCH – WEDNESDAY EVENING.

KNOCK KNOCK

FRIAR LAURENCE!

THAT SOUNDS LIKE FRIAR JOHN, BACK FROM MANTUA.

WHAT DID ROMEO SAY?

I WENT TO FIND ANOTHER FRIAR TO GO WITH ME. I MET UP WITH HIM AS HE WAS VISITING THE SICK; BUT THE TOWN OFFICIALS THOUGHT WE MIGHT SPREAD DISEASE AND LOCKED US IN THE HOUSE. I WASN'T ALLOWED TO LEAVE, SO I DIDN'T MAKE IT TO MANTUA.

WHO TOOK MY LETTER TO ROMEO?

NO ONE. I COULDN'T EVEN GET SOMEONE TO BRING IT BACK TO YOU.

OH NO!

IT WAS IMPORTANT THAT ROMEO RECEIVED THIS LETTER.

THIS WILL CAUSE MANY, MANY PROBLEMS! FRIAR JOHN, FETCH ME A CROWBAR.

I WILL.

I'LL HAVE TO GO TO THE TOMB ALONE. JULIET WILL WAKE UP IN THREE HOURS' TIME.

SHE CAN STAY HERE UNTIL I CAN GET ROMEO TO COME FOR HER.

THAT POOR LIVING CORPSE LOCKED UP INSIDE THAT TOMB!

141

143

147

149

153

IT WILL BE A WHILE BEFORE WE GET THE FULL STORY OF WHAT HAPPENED HERE.

THE PIAZZA, VERONA – EARLY THURSDAY MORNING.

BRING *OUT* THE SUSPECTS.

I AM THE ONE UNDER THE MOST SUSPICION.

I CONDEMN MYSELF, BUT WISH TO EXPLAIN.

TELL US WHAT YOU **KNOW**.

I'LL BE **BRIEF**. ROMEO AND **JULIET** WERE **MARRIED** TO EACH OTHER.

I PERFORMED THE MARRIAGE **CEREMONY**. LATER THAT DAY, **TYBALT** WAS **KILLED** – AND ROMEO WAS **FORCED** TO LEAVE VERONA.

JULIET WAS CRYING FOR ROMEO, *NOT* FOR TYBALT.

155

YOU THOUGHT **MARRYING** HER TO **PARIS** WOULD **HELP** HER, BUT IT ONLY MADE HER **WORSE**.

SHE **CAME** TO ME FOR A WAY **OUT** OF THAT WEDDING. SHE SAID SHE'D **KILL** HERSELF IF I DIDN'T **HELP** HER.

I GAVE HER A SLEEPING **POTION** WHICH MADE HER **APPEAR** TO BE **DEAD**.

THE **PLAN** WAS FOR **ROMEO** TO COME **BACK** WHEN THE POTION **WORE OFF**, AND FOR THEM TO LIVE IN **MANTUA** UNTIL IT WAS **SAFE** FOR THEM TO **RETURN** TO VERONA.

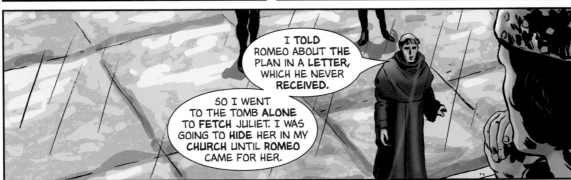

I **TOLD** ROMEO ABOUT **THE** PLAN IN A **LETTER**, WHICH HE NEVER **RECEIVED**.

SO I WENT TO THE TOMB **ALONE** TO **FETCH** JULIET. I WAS GOING TO **HIDE** HER IN MY **CHURCH** UNTIL **ROMEO** CAME FOR HER.

WHEN I **GOT** THERE, I FOUND **ROMEO** AND PARIS ALREADY **DEAD**. JULIET **WOKE**, BUT SHE WOULDN'T **LEAVE** THE TOMB WITH ME.

I RAN **AWAY** BEFORE THE **GUARDS** ARRIVED, AND IT LOOKS LIKE SHE **KILLED** HERSELF.

THAT'S **ALL** I CAN **TELL** YOU. JULIET'S **NURSE** WAS **AWARE** OF THIS MARRIAGE.

IF YOU THINK I AM TO **BLAME** FOR **ANY** OF THIS, THEN LET ME BE **EXECUTED**.

YOU'RE AN HONEST AND HOLY MAN, FRIAR.

WHAT DOES ROMEO'S MAN HAVE TO SAY?

I TOOK THE NEWS OF JULIET'S DEATH TO ROMEO. WE RODE QUICKLY FROM MANTUA TO THIS GRAVEYARD.

I HAVE A LETTER HERE, THAT ROMEO WANTED HIS FATHER TO HAVE.

GIVE ME THE LETTER.

WHERE IS COUNT PARIS'S PAGE?

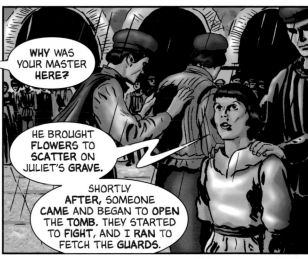

WHY WAS YOUR MASTER HERE?

HE BROUGHT FLOWERS TO SCATTER ON JULIET'S GRAVE.

SHORTLY AFTER, SOMEONE CAME AND BEGAN TO OPEN THE TOMB. THEY STARTED TO FIGHT, AND I RAN TO FETCH THE GUARDS.

THIS LETTER CONFIRMS THE FRIAR'S STORY.

ROMEO BOUGHT POISON AND USED IT TO KILL HIMSELF IN JULIET'S TOMB.

CAPULET! MONTAGUE!

DO YOU SEE THE DAMAGE CAUSED BY YOUR HATRED FOR EACH OTHER?

BOTH YOUR CHILDREN HAVE BEEN KILLED – I HAVE ALSO LOST TWO MEMBERS OF MY FAMILY.

WE HAVE ALL BEEN PUNISHED!

# Romeo & Juliet

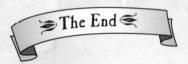

The End

# William Shakespeare

(c.1564 – 1616 AD)

Shakespeare is, without question, the world's most famous playwright. Yet, despite his fame, very few records and artefacts exist for him — we don't even know the exact date of his birth! April 23rd 1564 (St George's Day) is taken to be his birthday, as this was three days before his baptism (for which we do have a record). Records also tell us that he died on the same date in 1616, aged fifty-two.

The life of William Shakespeare can be divided into three acts.

### Act One – Stratford-upon-Avon

William was the eldest son of tradesman John Shakespeare and Mary Arden, and the third of eight children (he had two older sisters). The Shakespeares were a respectable family. The year after William was born, John (who made gloves and traded leather) became an alderman of Stratford-upon-Avon, and four years later he became High Bailiff (or mayor) of the town.

Little is known of William's childhood. He learnt to read and write at the local primary school, and later is believed to have attended the local grammar school, where he studied Latin and English Literature. In 1582, aged eighteen, William married a local farmer's daughter, Anne Hathaway. Anne was eight years his senior and three months pregnant. During their marriage they had three children: Susanna, born on

26th May 1583 and twins, Hamnet and Judith, born on 2nd February 1585. Hamnet (William's only son) died in 1596, aged eleven, from Bubonic Plague.

### Act Two – London

Five years into his marriage, in 1587, William's wife and children stayed in Stratford, while he moved to London. He appeared as an actor at *The Theatre* (England's first permanent theatre) and gave public recitals of his own poems; but it was his playwriting that created the most interest. His fame soon spread far and wide. When Queen Elizabeth I died in 1603, the new King James I (who was already King James VI of Scotland) gave royal consent for Shakespeare's acting company, *The Lord Chamberlain's Men* to be called *The King's Men* in return for entertaining the court. This association was to shape a

number of plays, such as *Macbeth*, which was written to please the Scottish King.

William Shakespeare is attributed with writing and collaborating on 38 plays, 154 sonnets and 5 poems, in just twenty-three years between 1590 and 1613. No original manuscript exists for any of his plays, making it hard to accurately date any of them. Printing was still in its infancy, and plays tended to change as they were performed. Shakespeare would write manuscript for the actors and continue to refine them over a number of performances. The plays we know today have survived from written copies taken at various stages of each play and usually written by the actors from memory. This has given rise to variations in texts of what is now known as "quarto" versions of the plays, until we reach the first official printing of each play in the 1623 *"folio" Mr William Shakespeare's Comedies, Histories, & Tragedies*. His last solo-authored work was *The Tempest* in 1611, which was only followed by collaborative work on two plays (*Henry VIII* and *Two Noble Kinsmen*) with John Fletcher. Shakespeare is strongly associated with the famous *Globe Theatre*. Built by his troupe in 1599, it became his "spiritual home", with thousands of people crammed into the small space for each performance. There were 3,000 people in the building in 1613 when a cannon-shot during a performance of *Henry VIII* set fire to the thatched roof and the entire theatre was burnt to the ground. Although it was rebuilt a year later, it marked an end to Shakespeare's writing and to his time in London.

## Act Three - Retirement

Shortly after the 1613 accident at *The Globe*, Shakespeare left the capital and returned to live once more with his family in Stratford-upon-Avon. He died on April 23rd 1616 and was buried two days later at the Church of the Holy Trinity (the same church where he had been baptised fifty-two years earlier). The cause of his death remains unknown.

## Epilogue

At the time of his death, Shakespeare had substantial properties, which he bestowed on his family and associates from the theatre. He had no son to inherit his wealth, and he left the majority of his possessions to his eldest daughter Susanna. Curiously, the only thing that he left to his wife Anne was his second-best bed! (although she continued to live in the family home after his death). William Shakespeare's last direct descendant died in 1670. She was his granddaughter, Elizabeth.

# Shakespeare Birthplace Trust

As so few relics survive from Shakespeare's life, it is amazing that the house where he was born and raised remains intact. It is owned and cared for by the Shakespeare Birthplace Trust, which looks after a number of houses in the area:

- Shakespeare's Birthplace.
- Mary Arden's Farm: The childhood home of Shakespeare's mother.
- Anne Hathaway's Cottage: The childhood home of Shakespeare's wife.
- Hall's Croft: The home of Shakespeare's eldest daughter, Susanna.
- New Place: Only the grounds exist of the house where Shakespeare died in 1616.
- Nash's House: The home of Shakespeare's granddaughter.

Shakespeare's Birthplace

www.shakespeare.org.uk

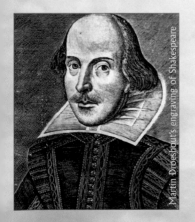

Martin Droeshout's engraving of Shakespeare

Formed in 1847, the Trust also works to promote Shakespeare around the world. In early 2009, it announced that it had found a new Shakespeare portrait, believed to have been painted within his lifetime, with a trail of provenance that links it to Shakespeare himself.

It is accepted that Martin Droeshout's engraving (left) that appears on the First Folio of 1623 is an authentic likeness of Shakespeare because the people involved in its publication would have personally known him. This new portrait (once owned by Henry Wriothesley, 3rd Earl of Southampton, one of Shakespeare's most loyal supporters) is so similar in all facial aspects that it is now suspected to have been the source that Droeshout used for his famous engraving.

www.shakespearefound.org.uk

# History of the Play

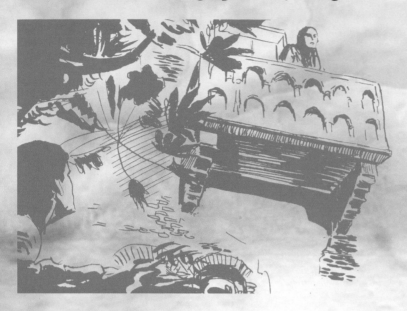

The tale of ill-fated love between Romeo and Juliet is intrinsically linked with Shakespeare, with the famous "balcony scene" providing some of his most enduring phrases:

*"But, soft! What light through yonder window breaks?*
*It is the east, and Juliet is the sun!"* (p55)

*"O Romeo, Romeo! Wherefore art thou Romeo?"* (p56)

*"What's in a name? That which we call a rose, by any other word would smell as sweet;"* (p56)

However, as with the vast majority of his works, Shakespeare's play is an adaptation of a story that already existed (*The Tempest* is his only play without a clear source).

Stories of frustrated love are as old as civilisation itself and can be found even in ancient myths. The first recognisable form of *Romeo*

*and Juliet* appeared around 1460 by Masuccio Salernitano. In it, Mariotto Mignanelli and Gianozza Saraceni of Siena fall in love and are married in secret by a friar. Shortly afterwards, Mariotto quarrels, fights with and kills a noble citizen. Mariotto is banished from the town, and Gianozza is forced into marriage by her father (who is unaware of her marriage with Mariotto). The friar creates a potion for Gianozza that makes her appear dead, and she is taken to the family tomb. From there, the friar escorts her to husband, who receives word of her death before she can reach him. Mariotto returns to Siena, where he is seized and executed. Gianozza shuts herself away in a convent and soon dies from grief.

Salernitano's story became the inspiration for Luigi da Porto's *Giulietta e Romeo*. Da Porto set the story in Verona, where he was inspired by the two castles just outside the city, each owned by

a different family: the Capuleti and the Montecchi, thus introducing the notion of the feuding families. The ending is more tragic than Shakespeare's, with Romeo killing himself by the side of Giulietta, but seeing her revive in his final moments.

In 1554, an Italian writer by the name of Matteo Bandello published his own version of *Giulietta e Romeo*. This story was much more popular than its predecessors. Not only was it translated into English but, importantly for Shakespeare, it became the basis of a 3,020-line poem by Arthur Brooke called *The Tragicall Historye of Romeus and Juliet* (1562). Brooke's poem has all the main characters, albeit with some spelling differences: Romeus Montagew, Juliet Capilet, Prince Escalus, Tybalt, Paris, Friar Lawrence, Juliet's nurce [sic] and even Peter (although he is cited as one of Romeus's men).

Although Shakespeare embellished the story (and of course added his beautiful language) the events can all be found in Brooke's poem — even Friar John being unable to deliver the message to Romeus because of quarantine. It is possible that Shakespeare worked with other sources, too. He may have read the French translation of Bandello's novel, as well as an English version of the story by William Painter called *Palace of Pleasure.* Yet it is Brooke's poem that most closely matches the Bard's great play, as shown in the excerpt, opposite, in which Juliet discovers the name of her new love as the guests leave the masked ball.

## The Tragicall Historye of Romeus and Juliet
### by Arthur Brooke (1562)

As carefull was the mayde what way were best deuise
To learne his name, that intertaind her in so gentle wise.
Of whome her hart receiued so deepe, so wyde a wounde,
An auncient dame she calde to her, and in her eare gan rounde.
This olde dame in her youth, had nurst her with her mylke,
With slender nedle taught her sow, and how to spin with silke.
What twayne are those (quoth she) which prease vnto the doore,
Whose pages in theyr hand doe beare, two toorches light before.
And then as eche of them had of his houshold name,
So she him namde yet once agayne the yong and wyly dame.
And tell me who is he with vysor in his hand
That yender doth in masking weede besyde the window stand.
His name is Romeus (sayd she) a Montegewe.
Whose fathers pryde first styrd the strife which both your
houscholdes rewe.
The woord of Montegew, her ioyes did ouerthrow,
And straight in steade of happy hope, dyspayre began to growe.
What hap haue I quoth she, to loue my fathers foe?
What, am I wery of my wele? what, doe I wishe my woe?
But though her grieuous paynes distraind her tender hart,
Yet with an outward shewe of ioye she cloked inward smart.
And of the courtlyke dames her leaue so courtly tooke,
That none dyd gesse the sodain change by changing of her looke.

Shakespeare contracted the nine months of events within the poem into just five days. While that adds to the tension of the play in performance, it is likely to have been a conscious and practical decision to tailor the story for the stage, as the passing of time is hard to capture in theatre.

The play appeared in print for the first time (the *First Quarto*) in 1597. The introduction of that edition tells us that it had already been performed by the time it was published:

*An Excellent conceited Tragedie of Romeo and Iuliet, As it hath been often (with great applause) plaid publiquely, by the Honourable the L. of Hunsdon and his Seruants.*

It was written before the *Globe Theatre* was built (1599), in the reign of Elizabeth I (which ended in 1603), while Shakespeare was writing for *The Lord Chamberlain's Men*.

### The Lord Chamberlain's Men
Until the 1660s, the law prevented women and girls from acting. All parts, even Juliet, were played by males!

Even though Shakespeare's plays were hugely popular, only sparse records exist of actual performances. The earliest official recording of a production of *Romeo and Juliet* doesn't occur until as late as 1662, in a theatre in Lincoln's Inn Fields. The famous diarist Samuel Pepys attended the opening night and thought very poorly of it:

*"It is a play of itself the worst that I have ever heard in my life, and the worst acted that I ever saw these people do; and am resolved to go no more to see the first time of acting, for they were all of them out more or less."*

Despite that early criticism, *Romeo and Juliet* remains one of Shakespeare's best-loved plays, being performed regularly throughout the world, as well as being adapted into other media: classical music (*Berlioz* [1839] and *Tchaikovsky* [1870]), opera (*Gounod* [1867]), ballet (*Prokofiev* [1935]), musical (Leonard Bernstein's *West Side Story* [1957]), movie (many!), and, of course, this graphic novel.

# Page Creation

| 167. | **Large Night.** Romeo approaches the balcony and sees Juliet. | | |
|---|---|---|---|
| | Original Text | Plain Text | Quick Text |
| ROMEO (TH) | But, soft! what light through yonder window breaks? It is the east, and Juliet is the sun! Arise, fair sun, and kill the envious moon, Who is already sick and pale with grief, That thou, her maid, art far more fair than she, | But, soft! what light through yonder window breaks? It is the east, and Juliet is the sun! Arise, fair sun, and kill the envious moon, that is pale and sad because you, Juliet, are more beautiful. | But, soft! what light through yonder window breaks? It is the east, and Juliet is the sun! Arise, fair sun, and kill the moon. |
| 168. | Juliet's POV from the balcony. She's looking up wistfully at the moon, not down at the ground. She doesn't see Romeo. He stares up at her. | | |
| ROMEO (TH) | Be not her maid, since she is envious; Her vestal livery is but sick and green, And none but fools do wear it; cast it off. | Don't worry about the moon's jealousy. It is sick and green – the colour of fools and virgins. Get rid of it! | It is jealous of your beauty. |
| 168b | | | |
| ROMEO (TH) | It is my lady; O! it is my love: O, that she knew she were! She speaks, yet she says nothing: what of that? Her eye discourses, I will answer it. | It is my lady; Oh! it is my love. Oh, I wish she knew that I love her. She speaks, but says nothing. It doesn't matter – her eyes do the talking, and I'll answer them! | She is my love! |
| (+silent panel) | | | |
| 169. | Juliet looks down and Romeo ducks for cover. | | |
| ROMEO (TH) | I am too bold, 'tis not to me she speaks: Two of the fairest stars in all the heaven, Having some business, do entreat her eyes To twinkle in their spheres till they return. What if her eyes were there, they in her head? The brightness of her cheek would shame those stars, As daylight doth a lamp; | I'm being overconfident. She's not talking to me. Two of the brightest stars in the sky have asked her eyes to take their place for a while. Imagine if her eyes were in the sky and the stars were in her head? The beauty of her face would outshine these stars, like the sun outshines a lamp. | She seems to be speaking – – but not to me. Her eyes are like stars! |
| 170. | Romeo peers out from his hiding place beneath the balcony. Juliet is looking away across the garden, resting her head on her hand. | | |
| | Original Text | Plain Text | Quick Text |
| ROMEO (TH) | her eyes in heaven, Would through the airy region stream so bright, That birds would sing and think it were not night. See, how she leans her cheek upon her hand! O! that I were a glove upon that hand, That I might touch that cheek! | If her eyes were up in the sky, they'd shine so bright, the birds would think it was morning and begin singing. See how she's leaning her cheek on her hand I wish I was a glove on that hand, so that I could touch that cheek! | – She is so beautiful, leaning her cheek on her hand, so that I could touch that cheek. |

Page 55 from the script of *Romeo & Juliet* showing the three text versions.

## 1. Script

The first stage in creating a graphic novel adaptation of a Shakespeare play is to split the original script into comic book panels, describing the images to be drawn as well as the dialogue and any captions. To do this, not only does the script writer need to know the play well, but he also needs to visualise each page in his head as he writes the art descriptions for each panel (there are over 600 panels in *Romeo and Juliet*).

Once this is created, the dialogue is adapted into Plain Text and Quick Text to create the three versions of the book, which all use the same artwork.

## 2. Character Sheets

Because *Romeo and Juliet* is such a well-known play, Will Volley needed very little time to familiarise himself with the characters. However, an artist still needs to "climb into the story" while deciding on the right approach for the artwork. Here you can see Will's designs for Romeo and Juliet, which we instantly agreed upon. The whole process moves steadily towards bringing the play to life and, suddenly, the names "Romeo" and "Juliet" are no longer simply names in a script — they have turned into actual people!

## 3. Rough Sketch

The rough sketch created from the script.

Armed with the character visualisations, the artist begins work on the 152 pages required for the book. Each page is first sketched out quickly in order to check panel layouts, ensure there is enough space for the lettering, explore continuity elements and to establish the pacing of the action. Will's roughs are very descriptive. As you can see here, he is already considering the lighting of the scenes, how the shadows will fall across surfaces, and so on. These rough layouts are then sent to the editor for approval. If any changes need to be made, it is far easier to make them at this stage from the fast rough layouts than to make changes to finished linework.

## 4. Linework

The process to create the finished artwork begins as soon as the editor agrees to the rough sketch. The artwork is created on A3 art board at approximately 150% of the finished printed size. That magnification allows more freedom when creating the linework and makes for a better final image. As the linework is reduced, it has the effect of "tightening" the art, improving the overall look of the page.

Interestingly, the rough sketch details some artistic elements that won't be tackled until the colouring stage. For example, the sketchy colouring on the sides of faces due to the moonlit scene doesn't appear in the linework because it only deals in stark black and white (and Will doesn't use a technique called "feathering" which is the traditional way to render a curved surface in black and white artwork). Certain textures are added at this stage, such as the folds in the clothing and the rendering of materials, like the stone of the balcony and wall.

The inked image, ready to be coloured.

The final coloured artwork.

The finished page 55 with Quick Text lettering.

## 5. Colouring

Adding colour really brings the page and its characters to life. There is far more to the colouring stage than simply replacing the white areas with flat colour. Some of the linework itself is shaded, while great emphasis is placed upon texture and light sources to get realistic shadows and highlights. Effects are also considered, such as the glow coming from the light in Juliet's bedroom. Finally, the whole page is colour-balanced to the other pages of that scene, and to the overall book.

## 6. Lettering

The final stage is to add the captions, sound effects, and speech bubbles from the script. These are placed on top of the finished, coloured pages. Three versions of each page are lettered, one for each of the three versions of the book (Original Text, Plain Text and Quick Text).

### Original Text
ISBN: 978-1-906332-19-8

### Plain Text
ISBN: 978-1-906332-20-4

### Quick Text
ISBN: 978-1-906332-21-1

# Teaching Resource Packs

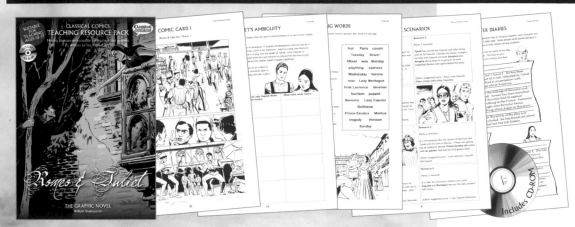

To accompany each title in our series of graphic novels and to help with their application in the classroom, we also publish teaching resource packs. These widely acclaimed 100+ page books are spiral-bound, making the pages easy to photocopy. They also include a CD-ROM with the pages in PDF format, ideal for whole-class teaching on whiteboards, laptops, etc or for direct digital printing. These books are written by teachers, for teachers, helping students to engage in the play or novel. Suitable for teaching ages 10-17, each book provides exercises that cover structure, listening, understanding, motivation and character as well as key words, themes and literary techniques. Although the majority of the tasks focus on the use of language and comprehension, there are also many cross-curriculum topics, covering areas within history, ICT, drama, reading, speaking, writing and art. An extensive Educational Links section provides further study opportunities. Devised to encompass a broad range of skill levels, they provide many opportunities for differentiated teaching and the tailoring of lessons to meet individual needs.

"Thank you! These will be fantastic for all our students. It is a brilliant resource and to have the lesson ideas too are great. Thanks again to all your team who have created these."
*B.P. KS3*

"As to the resource, I can't wait to start using it! Well done on a fantastic service."
*Will*

"...you've certainly got a corner of East Anglia convinced that this is a fantastic way to teach and progress English literature and language!"
*Chris Mehew*

## OUR RANGE OF TEACHING RESOURCE PACKS AVAILABLE

*Romeo & Juliet*
978-1-906332-39-6

*Macbeth*
978-1-907127-01-4

*Henry V*
978-1-907127-00-7

*The Tempest*
978-1-906332-40-2

*Frankenstein*
978-1-907127-03-8

*Jane Eyre*
978-1-907127-02-1

*A Christmas Carol*
978-1-907127-04-5

*Great Expectations*
978-1-906332-13-6

- Only **£19.99** each

- 100+ Spiral-bound, photocopiable pages.

- Electronic version included for whole-class teaching and digital printing.

- Cross-curricular topics and activities.

- Ideal for differentiated teaching.

# ALL SHAKESPEARE TITLES ARE AVAILABLE IN THREE TEXT VERSIONS

| | |
|---|---|
| Original Text | THE ENTIRE SHAKESPEARE PLAY - UNABRIDGED! |
| Plain Text | THE ENTIRE PLAY TRANSLATED INTO PLAIN ENGLISH! |
| Quick Text | THE ENTIRE PLAY IN QUICK MODERN ENGLISH FOR A FAST-PACED READ! |

## Macbeth: The Graphic Novel

• Script Adaptation: John McDonald • Pencils: & Inks: Jon Haward • Inking Assistant: Gary Erskine • Colours & Letters: Nigel Dobbyn

144 Pages • £9.99

ISBN: 978-1-906332-03-7     ISBN: 978-1-906332-04-4     ISBN: 978-1-906332-05-1

## The Tempest: The Graphic Novel

• Script Adaptation: John McDonald • Pencils: Jon Haward • Inks: Gary Erskine • Colours: & Letters: Nigel Dobbyn     144 Pages • £9.99

ISBN: 978-1-906332-29-7     ISBN: 978-1-906332-30-3     ISBN: 978-1-906332-31-0

## Henry V: The Graphic Novel

• Script Adaptation: John McDonald • Pencils: Neill Cameron • Inks: Bambos • Colours: Jason Cardy & Kat Nicholson • Letters: Nigel Dobbyn

144 Pages • £9.99

ISBN: 978-1-906332-00-6     ISBN: 978-1-906332-01-3     ISBN: 978-1-906332-02-0

FOR MORE DETAILS AND ORDERING INFORMATION VISIT: www.classicalcomics.com